Cyrus the Far Sighted One

Laurie Montemurro

Cyrus the Far Sighted One

Radical Bookshop and Press
4838 Richard Road SW, Suite 300
Calgary, AB T3E 6L1

FIC029000 – Fiction, Short Stories

Chinook Blast Collection
Volume 1
February 1, 2021

Editors: Lexie Angelo
Cover Design: Lexie Angelo

ISBN-13: 978-1-990201-06-6

Printed in the United States

Typeset in Merriweather

contents

Cyrus the Far Sighted One

Ten coins today. Twenty dollars. They clink together with such a satisfying sound. There is a coin for every hour Cyrus has spent prostrate on the pavement, arm extended in supplication. Toronto is a city of tall buildings, power, wealth, and many, many poor people. Today ten powerful people have paused long enough in their journey to drop a coin in his hand. Cyrus feels blessed with his earnings, he bows his head and mumbles a brief prayer to his mother. She must be watching over his journey in this wretched world. He has a family, a job, a lover and he can make choices in his life. Not everyone can say that. Finishing his prayer, he squats in front of an old brownstone building, well out of the way of the foot traffic, to consider his options.

His first desire is to buy paper and a pencil to compose a poem to his beloved, a young man with sweet hazel eyes that gaze into his with such compassion it leaves him feeling raw with desire. He has taken to meeting his lover in the park at morning's first light, their coupling a reminder of what being alive means. He could slide the poem under his lover's door, walk home in moonlight through quiet streets with the joy of morning's sweet promise flooding his soul.

Or he could buy vanilla candles and go to the church and light them in memory of his mother. He imagines the sound of her soft voice washing through his prayers, blessing him for honouring her memory.

Another choice could be a visit to the public baths, a rare indulgence indeed. Cyrus squints to remember the last time he bathed. Laughing, he twirls his fingers on the sidewalk, why should he bathe when he is surrounded by dust? No sooner clean then the street dirt, in this city of millions would settle on him. No, he thinks, it is better to blend in with everyone else. Being tidy attracts attention, the kind that ends in a beating and the loss of his hard-earned coins.

Besides, Raicheal, his wife of ten years, would be suspicious if he came home clean. "I used to bathe every day at home with my family," she likes to remind him. For Cyrus to show up scented and scrubbed, well, that would be insulting to the woman who gave up her status in a wealthy family from High Park. "I used to smell like soap and citrus fruit, now I smell like you – a failure."

Cyrus knows that his once handsome wife no longer loves him. The attention of his male lover soothes his need for physical intimacy, but he believes it is Raicheal who is his true soulmate. It is his failure as a businessman that resulted in their quick slide into the slums of Danforth, his begging, her pride at not telling her family, all of which have wriggled like black worms into their love. Now only accusing stares and muttered insults meet him at the door.

But ten coins today! It is a wealth of riches for a beggar, especially one who still has all of his limbs intact. The coins clink gently in his pocket as he stands, they sing of possibility. "See Raicheal," he imagines chortling as he walks through the door, "It is not only the rich who have choices!"

Cyrus likes this comfort of belief in his freedom to choose how to spend his earnings. It allows him to stand tall amongst his fellow beggars, although not too tall. He has learned showing pride as a beggar results in fewer coins at the end of the day which results in fewer choices. It is a delicate balance, he reflects, allowing himself to feel a man's pride while having to stoop low to keep his place in the Beggar's Accord. There is only one street where the Accord is allowed, and it is among the streets where the powerful business elite of Toronto work. Spots are precious and he had to pass a rigorous interview before he was allocated a place on the corner of Bloor and Perth. A meek attitude is necessary for the job and Cyrus was determined to keep his spot and his good standing with the Accord.

Decision made, Cyrus strides forward, heart soaring in the late afternoon light, to the Allan Gardens outdoor market. A few of the stall keepers there indulge him as he sorts through their bruised produce in exchange for four coins and a verse. Words roll off his tongue like the beets and onions through his fingers as he tries to honour the sellers, extolling the virtue of their wares, even if it is only the rubbish he is allowed. Once the exchange of food and coin and words are complete and everyone is smiling, he moves on to his last stall.

Cyrus checks his coins to make sure he has enough to buy grain, by far the most important food for his family. The grain merchant never offers a special deal, no matter how sweet his smile or how complimentary his words. One day, Cyrus brought his daughter, Estella, hoping the child's sweet face and shy smile would ring a chord of charity in the merchant. But his effort was unsuccessful, and the merchant's heart remained as hard as his wooden ladle.

He moves quickly now, the afternoon is fading into evening and the market will close soon. Raicheal will be angry if there is no grain to cook and he will suffer an evening of her unrelenting lament of his unending failures. *Maybe I should have bought the paper and pencil after all?* His lover's face rises in his right eye while the image of his sweet, shy Estella comes to his left. He cannot bear the thought of his sweet little girl child going to bed with her belly empty. He blinks his eyes to clear them and heads to the grain stall.

Cyrus waits in line behind men he recognizes, fellow beggars from work. All of them past their youth, standing patiently. The men stand with their eyes cast down, mouths closed, keeping their dreams to themselves. Cyrus joins them, humming quietly, his thoughts flit between his lover's smiling eyes and his daughter's sweet face. *Yes, I am truly blessed to have both in my life.*

Cyrus is the last in line. He steps forward, looking slightly to the right and down of the merchant's face. He requests the same amount of grain he requests every evening. The merchant's greedy blue eyes are sly as he measures the amount into a paper sac. He holds it above the counter, just out of reach and names the price. Cyrus's head jerks up, "What?"

The merchant grins broadly at Cyrus's shock. "Grain prices doubled today. The US closed their borders to all trade due to civil war. Take it or leave it but hurry and make up your mind."

Cyrus stands bewildered, *why did I not hear of this today on the street? How can I afford enough to feed my family tonight? What will Raicheal say?* He feels his heart shrivel and the skin sags on his face. The remaining coins feel so few clutched in his hand, a ball of panic rises in his throat. The merchant's voice cuts through, "It is time to close, hurry up."

Cyrus mumbles, "I'll take half that measure." Laughing, a high shrill sound in the evening air, the merchant re-measures the grain and hands the small sac over the counter. Taking his coins, the fat merchant leans over and whispers, "You know, there are other ways to make money. I hear there is a black market for eyes in Gledhill Park. You could make enough to buy a full measure of grain for a couple of weeks."

"Sell an eye?" Cyrus knew of this practise but had never considered it for himself.

The merchant leans over the stall and jabs a finger into Cyrus's left cheek, "One less eye might come in handy at work."

Turning, the merchant slams the stall shutter down with a loud crash, leaving Cyrus to stare horrified at the warped red metal slats.

A pack of dogs run past, barking loudly, jolting him into movement. Stumbling along, shoulders slumped, head down, Cyrus thinks on what the merchant said. He knows men working the streets who sold an eye and fed their family for a month. For some, the resulting loss meant more coins at the end of the day, for others the gaping holes and seeping wounds worked to drive people away. He moans. *My body, this is all I own. To parcel it up and sell it off, what kind of man does that?*

At home, Raicheal is unusually quiet. She stares past him while he tells her the story of the grain, leaving out the merchant's suggestion of selling an eye. When he is done his story, she sniffs and turns away, chops the few vegetables and cooks them with the grain for their meagre dinner. Cyrus sits, waiting for Estella to plea for stories and tug on his arm for him to join her games. But the room remains quiet. Estella ignores him and Raicheal refuses to look at him. His earlier joy has vanished, the ten coins no longer an achievement.

When the meal is ready, Raicheal serves only Estella and herself.

"Where is my food?" Cyrus asks. Normally he is served the largest portion first.

Her gaze sweeps past him and she sniffs. "Maybe you should work harder so that you can eat with us. Why should I stay with you if you can't even properly feed the family?" Then staring right into his soft brown eyes with her hard-gray gaze, "I am thinking of taking Estella to live with my parents."

Her words slam into him with the force of conviction. *What the merchant said is true, what use am I, a man who can't even provide enough food for my family?* Raicheal will leave me, take my child, I will be alone, a failure in everyone's eyes.

Silence blankets the room. It seems too soon that they are done eating. There should be more food. They should have to take more time. Cyrus's eyes fill with tears as Raicheal collects the bowls and walks out, his sweet Estella gripping his wife's large hand.

Cyrus sits on his wooden chair in the main room, staring at the bare walls. The long hours of dark fold into dawn. No one comes to ask why he sits there. No one offers a kind word, a gentle smile of encouragement. There is no coming together as a family to address this new challenge. He has to decide how much his family is worth to him.

With the arrival of dawn, Cyrus sits tall. *It is true, I do have parts a beggar could do without. I will sell one of them, proof that I know what is important as a father, a man. I can make more money on the street, provide for my family.* He turns his mind away from the image of Vlad, who had sold an eye to buy medicine for his child. The child died and now Vlad's eye oozes a constant stream of pink pus from beneath his patch. The sight is so off putting, people hurry past him, fearing they might catch a disease if they came too close. Vlad now huddles in a doorway at the far end of the street where few pass by.

Cyrus is determined to not let this happen. Some of the money he earns will go towards medicine so his eye will heal properly, and he can stay working on Bloor Street where the crowds are thickest. Maybe he can convince Raicheal to let him bring Estella. Her face might convince people to toss more coins into his hand. If he brings more money home, then Raicheal won't look past him as if he doesn't exist.

He will lose his lover. Cyrus swallows a sob, imagines his lover's face and folds the image away much like his lover carefully folds his poems and tucks them into his pocket, "For later." He has a family, and it is for them that he must provide.

Standing, Cyrus goes to the kitchen and drinks a glass of water. He washes his face to clean the grime away so the doctors can see the quality of his eyes. He leaves the house, deliberating which eye will be the better one to sell, the eye he can wink with or the eye that holds his family in sight. Perhaps the doctors will insist on making the choice, but he would like to be prepared if he is asked.

By the time he reaches the clinic there is a small line-up of men of all ages outside. They are quiet, breathing softly in the chill air. One stares defiantly around at the others, challenging anyone to question his being in line. The others gaze down, defeated at being brought to this place in order to survive. Cyrus stands at the back of the line, trying to feel brave and failing.

When the clinic door opens, there is no surge forward to get in. Soft shuffling and murmured voices carry outside as the men enter one by one. When Cyrus reaches the desk, he is greeted by a male nurse who asks him his name and age. The nurse takes a light and shines it in each of his eyes, instructing him to move his eyes from side to side and up and down. A note is made beside his name and he is asked to stand against the wall, he will be called when the doctors are ready. Cyrus has many questions, but the nurse is already calling for the next man, so he shuffles to the wall to stand with the others. No one talks.

Cyrus is led into a large well-lit room where cots are lined up in neat rows. Trays of small, shiny tools rest on carts ready to be rolled from one bed to the next. There is a sickly sweetish smell in the air, the hum of a fridge and the slightly louder hum of the doctors' voices as they instruct the men to lie down on the beds. Male nurses move among the cots, washing the men's faces with soap and drawing a circle around which eye is being sold. One man starts to cry, insisting in a high voice he has changed his mind. He runs out of the room. The others avert their gaze, undecided if he is the smart one for making that choice or not enough of a man to go through with it.

Cyrus is sweating. His belly is knotted and the small amount of water he drank that morning is making him feel sick. A nurse swabs his face with disinfectant, the black pen circles around his left eye. *No more holding my family in my sight all day.*

"Time to close your eyes. You'll feel a little prick and then numbness in the face."

"You'll put me out, right? I won't feel anything?"

"That is correct. Ready?"

Cyrus sees a needle descending and shuts his eyes. It hurts more than a prick. A soft weight is placed on his nose and he understands what the sweet smell in the air is from. He falls asleep.

Cyrus awakes to the sound of weeping and the smell of vomit. His face is numb though there is pain, a distant bellow of what is to come. His stomach heaves. He rolls over in time to vomit what little there is in his stomach into the pan placed on the floor. A nurse comes by to check on him and tells him he can leave when he is ready, his money will be waiting for him at the front. Cyrus realizes he doesn't even know how many coins he will receive from this sale of himself. He sits up and his head spins. He waits until the spinning slows then slowly shifts his weight onto his feet. His fingers brush an unfamiliar piece of cloth and twine, the patch. It sits on top of a gauze bandage. "Best to keep that clean if you want it to heal closed", the nurse says. "You can buy more gauze at the shop down the street and if you need it, something to kill the pain."

Cyrus whispers his thanks and shuffles out into the front room. He is dizzy and has a hard time seeing where to put his feet or how to gauge the space in front of him. His fingers stay in contact with the wall and he feels the greasy line where countless other hands have gone ahead, feeling their way back into street. The nurse at the front desk hands him a packet of coins. "There is a drugstore down the street. You can buy clean gauze and pain killers there. Keep it clean and you should be back at work in a couple of days."

"Thank you." His tongue is thick, and his mouth is dry. Those two words barely make it out of his mouth.

Outside the world is dusky, the day almost over. Cyrus looks at the slow-moving men on the street, all making their way to the shop to buy gauze and pills. *Maybe they all know Vlad, and no one wants to end up like him.* He follows the men into the shop and purchases the gauze but not the pills. They cost as much as food for three days. Cyrus decides his family's gratitude will be better than a pill to endure the pain. Besides, he has enough money that he won't have to work the street for a week, and he can rest, and let the wound heal.

Still shuffling like an old man, Cyrus moves through the dark streets towards his home. His head pounds. He struggles to balance on the cracked pavement. He could use the comfort of Raicheal's hand to guide him. Reaching his door, he notices through the pain the place is dark and quiet, there are no candles lit, no voices.

"Raicheal, Estella, I am home."

No answer.

Hand on the wall, Cyrus moves into the second room where they sleep then into the small closet they use as a bathroom. No one. It is then he notices the house is empty of not just his family, but of their belongings also. There is no mat on the floor, no blankets for sleeping, no clothes, no dishes, nothing. *She has gone back to her parents and taken everything.*

18

Leaning against the rough brick wall, Cyrus slides himself down to the floor. Tears are streaming down his face, the ache in his empty eye socket a mere echo of the pain encircling his heart. Cyrus curls himself into a tight ball, grasping the small packet of money in his hand.

"My family, my family," he sobs. "I have lost my family for a few coins."

ACKNOWLEDGEMENTS

Thank you Rose and Laurie for providing the nudges to move this story along.

ABOUT THE AUTHOR

Laurie is fairly new to the world of writing. She completed the University of Calgary's Creative Writing Certification program in December 2020 and is currently participating in Humber College's Creative Writing program. Prior to this desire to communicate through words, Laurie used movement to express her stories. She started her career as one of the founding members of Springboard Dance Collective in 1988, gradually moving on to work as an independent artist. Her works has been produced in Calgary, Millarville, Victoria, Vancouver, Edmonton, Saskatoon, Winnipeg, Toronto, Hornby Island, Denman Island, Cumberland and Courtenay.

This is her first published written story and she is very excited to be a part of this Radical Books series.

SPECIAL THANKS

Chinook Blast Festival

The City of Calgary

Tourism Calgary

Calgary Municipal Land Corporation

Calgary Arts Development

Calgary Public Library

IngramSpark